MOON'S FIRST FRIENDS

One Giant Leap for Friendship

words by **Susanna Leonard Hill**   pictures by **Elisa Paganelli**

sourcebooks
jabberwocky

The Moon was queen of the night sky.
  She was so bright that everything she touched glowed with silver light.
  But after many, many years had passed, she was lonely.
  "If only someone would visit me," she said.

"Hello, down there!" she called to the lumbering dinosaurs. "If you come up here, you won't feel so heavy—you'll feel lighter than air!"

But the dinosaurs stayed where they were.

Under the Moon's watchful eye, the surface of the Earth changed.
The Moon saw glorious new creatures come and go:

saber-toothed tigers,

mastodons,

woolly mammoths,

dodo birds,

whales,

rhinoceroses,

and elephants.

But they all stayed earthbound and rarely looked up to her in the night sky.

But then, she saw something new.
At night, people conjured fires like tiny stars.
"There are millions of stars for you up here," she offered.
But the people stayed where they were.

The Moon watched as she circled and circled the Earth. On the wide sweep of the hot Sahara, the Egyptians built stone pyramids that towered toward the sky.

"They're trying to reach me!" the Moon marveled.

But though the pyramids were mighty, they came nowhere near high enough to reach the Moon.

Perhaps they didn't see her.

She spun and twirled, from new moon to majestic silver pearl and back again, showing off for the people below.

But no one came.

She watched as down on Earth, people came up with all kinds of ways to get from one place to another.
But they did not sail,

or drive,

or cycle,

or float to the Moon.

Then, on a windy day in North Carolina, the first airplane flew above a beach.
"You're doing great!" encouraged the Moon. "You just need to fly a little higher!"

But the people on Earth only traveled to visit one another.
Was it possible they didn't know she was there?

At high noon, the Moon slipped purposefully between the Earth and the Sun, blocking all the daylight. Then she slid aside again, allowing the Sun to shine through. "No one could have missed that!" she thought.

But still, no one ventured away from Earth.
Would she ever have a visitor?

Just when the Moon was losing hope, the people on Earth began to experiment with rockets, and the Moon watched with great interest. But the humans still had a lot to learn.

One day, the Moon's hopes soared. A chimpanzee in a Mercury capsule rocketed toward her. A visitor! At last!

But, alas, he returned to Earth without reaching her.

And then, one hot July day, a tremendous rocket stood upon a launchpad with two small spaceships perched on top.
The countdown began!

At thirty stories high and weighing six million pounds, the rocket rose into the air amid an explosion of flames. Slowly at first, and then faster...and FASTER!

The rocket fell away in stages, but the
two spaceships hurtled toward the Moon.
"They're coming!" the Moon said.
"They're actually coming!"

One of the spaceships remained at a distance, circling.
But the other came closer...closer...until at last its spindle
legs touched down.

"Welcome!" she greeted the
men who emerged from the ship.

The astronauts walked across her surface with great bounding steps that made her dust bloom. They seemed delighted with how far they could travel with each stride.

The Moon gave them gifts of moon rocks and dust.

"Take these back to Earth," she said. "Then even though I can't visit you, a part of me will be there."

The men left her a present in return—a handsome plaque that read:

HERE MEN FROM THE PLANET EARTH
FIRST SET FOOT UPON THE MOON
JULY 1969, A.D.
WE CAME IN PEACE FOR ALL MANKIND

They also left her a beautiful flag with red and white stripes and a scattering of white stars on a blue background.

Too soon, the astronauts had to leave.
"Goodbye," the Moon said as their ship floated away into the starry distance. "Come back anytime!"

She sighed with happiness. At last, someone had visited.

And now she had hope that it would happen again
...and again.
Maybe one day YOU will visit her!

Mission Moon

NASA (National Aeronautics and Space Administration) was established July 29, 1958, and became operational October 1, 1958. NASA is part of the U.S. government and is in charge of science and technology related to airplanes and space. NASA makes satellites, sends probes into space, studies the solar system, explores planets and asteroids, and many other things. You probably know NASA best for its space program, which sends spacecrafts and people into space. Since its beginning, NASA has had many spaceflight programs, including Project Mercury, Project Apollo, the International Space Station, and more!

Out-of-this-world Facts

* It takes about one month—twenty-nine and a half days—for the Moon to get all the way around the Earth!

* The Moon does not give off light the way the Sun does. What we see as moonglow is actually the reflected light of the Sun.

* Earth's Moon is the fifth largest one in our solar system.

* The Moon is much smaller than the Earth—about one-fourth the Earth's size. The Moon is only 2,159 miles across from one side to the other (diameter), with a circumference of 6,783.5 miles. Earth's diameter is 7,926 miles. The Moon has no air, no weather, and no life, although water was discovered on the Moon in 2009.

Phases of the Moon

New Moon · Waxing Crescent · First Quarter · Waxing Gibbous · Full Moon · Waning Gibbous · Last Quarter · Waning Crescent

The Apollo 11 Voyage

On May 25, 1961, President John F. Kennedy went to Congress with a very special goal: American astronauts were going to visit the Moon in less than ten years! Although many people thought it couldn't be done, Congress liked the idea so much that they approved a budget of more than $25 billion. That's a lot of money!

NASA launched the Apollo 11 program with the goal of landing Americans on the Moon, taking samples, photos, and data, and then returning home safely. The program was challenging, and NASA estimated that it took over four hundred thousand engineers, scientists, and technicians to make the Moon landing possible. Finally, on July 16, 1969, after more than eight years of training, planning, and preparation, NASA launched the Saturn V rocket from Cape Kennedy.

Piloted by astronauts Neil Armstrong, Buzz Aldrin, and Michael Collins, Saturn V flew through space for more than three days. On July 20, 1969, more than 530 million people listened as Neil Armstrong became the first man to set foot on the Moon, saying, "...one small step for man, one giant leap for mankind." After almost twenty-two hours on the Moon's surface, Apollo 11 safely returned to Earth!

The Apollo 11 lunar landing crew participate in training for the mission. From left to right are Edwin (Buzz) Aldrin Jr., lunar module pilot; Neil Armstrong, commander; and Michael Collins, command module pilot. Image Credit: NASA.

Buzz Aldrin poses for a photograph beside the United States flag on the moon. Image Credit: NASA.

4.6 billion years ago – Earth begins forming from a cloud of gas and dust

3.8 billion years ago – First life begins

Hadean Era: 4.6 – 3.8 billion years ago

Archean Era: 3.8 – 2.5 billion years ago

4.5 billion years ago – The Moon forms

The Space Suit

Space is a beautiful place, but if you want to go there, you'll need the right clothes. In space, it's very, very cold, there isn't any sound, and there's no air. NASA designed special suits to keep their astronauts safe on their way to visit the Moon. For the Apollo 11 mission, each suit was specifically made for the astronauts, and each astronaut had three different suits. At $2 million each, that's quite an expensive wardrobe! An astronaut's suit has oxygen tanks to let them breathe in space, radios to communicate with each other (and even to Earth!), and protective gear to keep them safe while they travel through space.

The Rocket

Have you ever blown up a balloon and then let the air out? What happens? The air shoots out the opening, and the balloon shoots off in the other direction! Well, rockets work pretty much the same way. When a rocket is launched, its engines fire and exhaust gases blow out at high speed, pushing the rocket up and away.

The Saturn V rocket was built for the Apollo 11 mission, but in order to visit the Moon, the rocket had to first break free of Earth's gravity. The Earth's gravity is strong and likes to keep things on the ground.

Hi!

Pressure Helmet

Utility Pocket

Biomedical Access Flap

Lunar Boot

650 million years ago – Earth is covered in ice

370 million years ago – First amphibians evolve

Proterozoic Era: 2.5 billion – 540 million years ago

Paleozoic Era: 540 – 250 million years ago

475 million years ago – First land plants evolve

300 million years ago – Supercontinent Pangea forms

Thank goodness, or else you wouldn't be able to walk without floating off into the air! To escape Earth's gravity, a rocket needs engines strong enough to go almost eighteen thousand miles per hour. Going that fast requires a lot of fuel, so the Saturn V rocket was built with three "stages" that held the fuel. In total, the rocket was made of five main pieces: three fuel stages, the Instrument Unit and Command/Service Module, and the Lunar Module.

First Stage

The first stage is the big one on the ground. It uses almost five million pounds of fuel to get the rocket off the Earth and into the air, moving almost 7,500 feet per second! Have you ever watched a rocket launch on television? If so, this is probably what you saw.

Second Stage

Once Saturn V reached the upper atmosphere surrounding Earth, the booster engines and fuel tanks of the first stage broke off—but don't worry! This was all according to plan. Once all the fuel had been used to get off the ground, the astronauts didn't want to carry around all that extra weight, so they detached the parts they didn't need. This let them move faster while they started the second stage of their launch. The rockets for stage two were smaller, but they still used almost one million pounds of fuel and got the astronauts almost all the way to the Moon!

Third Stage

The third stage was a much smaller set of rockets, used by astronauts to get them into the Moon's orbit. After the boosters from the second stage broke off (just like the first!), the entire rocket was much smaller than when it started. This smaller craft required much less fuel to move through space and let the astronauts pilot it very carefully into the Moon's orbit. Once the astronauts were situated where they needed to be, the third stage broke off too! Now, with all three stages used up and detached, the only pieces that remained were the Instrument Unit and Command/Service Module, and the Lunar Module.

Instrument Unit and Command/Service Module

The Instrument Unit of Saturn V was the rocket's "brain." Using powerful computers, the Instrument Unit could do all the calculations required to get the astronauts safely to the Moon, and even autocorrect

225 million years ago – Dinosaurs evolve

200,000 years ago – Our species *Homo sapiens* evolves

175 million years ago – Pangea begins splitting into seven continents

14 million years ago – First great apes evolve

Mesozoic Era: 250 – 65 million years ago

Cenozoic Era: 65 million years ago – present

200 million years ago – Mammals evolve

65 million years ago – Flowering plants evolve

any problems that came up! This kept the astronauts safe and sound until they reached the Moon's orbit, where the pilots took over using the Command/Service Module. This module would be used to take the astronauts home but stayed in the Moon's orbit while the Lunar Module went to the Moon's surface.

Lunar Module

Now that they'd gone all the way from Earth to the Moon, all that the astronauts needed to do was land on the Moon's surface and say hello! Neil Armstrong and Buzz Aldrin detached from the Command/Service Module and flew down to the Moon's surface in the Lunar Module, officially becoming the Moon's first friends! This tiny spaceship could only hold two astronauts but had everything they needed to get onto the Moon, take their samples, photos, and videos, and then get back to the Command/Service Module.

The Long Trip Home

After the astronauts completed their mission on the Moon, it was time to say goodbye, but getting home was a mission in itself! They climbed back into their Lunar Module and used its tiny rockets to lift free of the Moon's surface. Once back in orbit, they reconnected with the Command/Service Module, which they had left behind with their fellow astronaut Michael Collins. After traveling back through space for more than four days, they finally reentered Earth's atmosphere and splashed down safely into the ocean. All their friends from NASA were eagerly waiting to hear everything about the Moon!

Apollo Spacecraft

Instrument Unit

Third Stage

Second Stage

First Stage

Scan this QR code to listen to Neil Armstrong's first words on the Moon!